My Fox Ate My Alarm Clock

David Blaze

For Zander...

Wow! That's Awesome!

Bird is the word!

CONTENTS

FRIDAY MORNING

I didn't feel safe at school. Sam sat behind me on the gym bleachers and blew spitballs at the back of my head. The big kid with a crew cut and a white tank top was Shane's best friend. He never forgave me for making the school bully go away.

"Everyone line up!" Coach Brown, the gym teacher, shouted. There were fifteen of us, boys and girls. Coach Brown wore a red workout jacket and a red cap. He had a clipboard in his hand and a whistle around his neck. He wasn't the nicest person in the world. He yelled at any kid that didn't move as fast as he wanted.

"Shane's coming for you, Jonah," Sam whispered from behind me. He laughed and jumped out of the bleachers to line up on the floor. I felt sick and thought about going to the front office to call my mom so she could take me home.

"Don't listen to him," Melissa told me, shaking her head. She was sitting right next to me. She wore a green sweatshirt and had her hair tied back in two ponytails. I was glad she was there because her smile made me feel better. "Shane didn't come to school today."

She was right. Miss Cox had called his name several times in English class that morning but he didn't answer. Today was the day he was supposed to return. I had looked all over the room, expecting Shane to pop his head up and attack me. He'd never forget the night he and his father were taken away by the police.

"Mr. Johnson?" Coach Brown said with his face right in front of mine. He called us by our last names. "I don't think you heard me." I realized I was still sitting down while everyone else was standing on the gym floor. I took a deep breath. Coach Brown was about to yell at me. "I said line up!" He blew his whistle as loud as he could. I wasn't sure if I'd ever hear anything again.

"We're doing the Presidential Fitness Program today and next week," he said. I saw the President on TV once. I wondered if he did any physical fitness or just made that program to torture us.

"Girls will go first," Coach Brown continued. He pointed at the metal pull-up bar on the other side of the gym. "I expect you to do at least three pull-ups." None of the girls moved. One of them shook her head and crossed her arms. Coach Brown blew his whistle and shouted, "Now! Move it!"

They ran to the other side. Coach Brown followed them. "I don't get paid enough for this," he muttered. He caught up to the girls and called them one at a time to the bar. I watched as some of them did two pull-ups. Some of them did one. And some did none at all — they just hung from the bar and fell down. I waited for Coach Brown to yell at them but he had a soft spot for girls. He shook his head and told them to go sit down.

Melissa was the last girl standing there. "Let's go, Miss Morgan," he said. "I'm not getting any younger." That was true. He was really old — like thirty.

Melissa jumped up and grabbed the bar. I didn't expect her to do any pull-ups. She was the nicest girl I knew and a good friend of mine. I didn't think she could hurt a fly. I stared in amazement as she did one pull-up. Two pull-ups. Three pull-ups. Four pull-ups!

Everyone cheered for her. I shouted, "That's right! That's how you do it!" Coach Brown smiled for the first time in his life and patted Melissa on the back. She ran over to me and smirked. "Did you see that?" she asked.

I nodded and high-fived her. "That was awesome. You're amazing, Melissa Morgan."

Sam laughed from behind me. "Jonah and Melissa sitting in a tree…"

My face felt like it was on fire. I couldn't breathe. I liked Melissa a lot but I didn't know how she felt about me. She giggled and sat down.

"Boys!" Coach Brown shouted. "It's your turn." He waved us toward the bar on the other side of the gym. "Let's do this."

We ran over to him as fast as we could. None of us wanted to be the last person because that person was the weakest. I was the third boy out of eight.

Sam pushed us out of the way and said, "I'll go first." He cracked his knuckles and moved his neck from side to side. "I can do this," he said out loud to himself. "I'm the man." He jumped up to the bar and did five pull ups!

He dropped down and rolled his shoulders back. "That's right," he said to us. "That's how a real man does it." Sam looked up at Coach Brown. "Right, Coach? I did five pull-ups and I only had to do three."

Coach Brown lowered his clipboard to his side. "Girls are supposed to do three." He took a deep breath and sighed. "Boys are supposed to do six." He pointed to the bleachers. "Go sit down."

A couple of guys laughed as Sam walked away with his head hung low. I couldn't laugh because five pull-ups were more than any of the girls could do. I had never done pull-ups before but they looked hard, like something you'd see on *American Ninja Warrior* on TV.

I let the other guys go before me, hoping we'd run out of time before I got to the metal bar. Some of the guys did six pull ups. Most of them could do three or four, like Melissa.

Before I knew it, I was the only person left. The pull-up bar was a mile high. I gulped. Coach Brown looked at his watch then stared at me like he had more important things to do. He waved his clipboard at the metal bar. "Let's go, Mr. Johnson. You can't do any worse than the girls."

My heart was racing. I couldn't move. I didn't want to be the one guy who couldn't do any pull-ups. The other guys would make fun of me for the rest of my life. I looked at the bleachers and realized no one was looking at me. They were talking and playing. Except for one person.

"You can do it, Joe!" Melissa shouted.

I smiled at her and nodded. I turned back to the bar. It was time to find out if I was the weakest link.

The gym doors opened with a loud crack that echoed through the room. Everyone became silent. I turned and saw the one face that made me wish I had gone home. It was Shane.

He walked straight toward me. His shoes made a deep clickety clack sound that made my heart beat faster with every step. He looked taller than the night the police took him away. He stopped right in front of me and hovered over me like the Eiffel Tower.

He didn't say anything. He wanted to show me that he was back and there was nothing I could do about it. He was the king.

"Mr. Connors!" Coach Brown shouted. "Why are you walking into my gym late? I hope you have a note." Shane pulled a note out of his pocket and handed it to the coach without ever taking his eyes off me. I didn't know where he had been for the last few months, but rumors were his dad went to jail. Had Shane gone to jail too? Maybe he was a hardened criminal now.

"Mr. Connors!" Coach Brown shouted again. "Show everyone how to do pull-ups the right way." Shane didn't move. "Now, Mr. Connors!"

Shane turned from me without saying anything. He stepped up to the metal bar and grabbed it without jumping up. I watched in amazement as he did nine pull-ups! A lot of kids on the bleachers were talking about how strong Shane was. And that they felt sorry for me.

Shane dropped to the floor and walked right back over to me. I was sure he was going to throw me to the ground like he did the first day we met. I closed my eyes. But nothing happened.

When I opened my eyes again, I saw Shane was on the bleachers, talking to Sam. No doubt they were planning how to destroy me.

"You're up, Mr. Johnson," Coach Brown said. "Make it

quick."

Sam and Shane were staring at me. Melissa was the only other person paying attention. I turned to the bar and took a deep breath. Here went nothing.

I jumped up and grabbed the bar. My fingers felt weird wrapped around it, like rubber bands. I held my breath and pulled myself up slowly to the bar, feeling it in my shoulders and upper back. It wasn't too bad. One pull-up done.

I went faster on the second one. It was easier that way. So then I did three. And four. Five. Six. Seven. Eight. Nine. This was too easy. I didn't understand why everyone else had trouble with this.

On my tenth pull-up, Coach Brown shouted, "Unseen force!" The room fell silent again. "Unseen force!"

I focused on the bar. Coach Brown counted out loud, shouting the numbers. "Eleven! Twelve! Thirteen! Fourteen! Fifteen! Sixteen! Seventeen!" They were getting harder to do. My shoulders were sore. I couldn't move as fast.

"Eighteen!" I wasn't sure I could do another one.

"Nineteen!" My back was on fire. I was breathing hard. Sweat fell from my face. There's no way I could do another one.

"Twenty!" I dropped down from the bar and rolled my shoulders back. They were sore but already getting stronger again. I had no idea where all that strength came from. I was not the weakest link.

A lot of the kids surrounded me and patted me on the back. They said things like, "That was dope!" and "Awesome!"

Melissa stood in front of me and smiled. "I knew you could do it, Joe."

We all turned when the gym doors cracked open again. I heard the clickety clack of Shane's shoes as the doors closed behind him. I was glad he left. Now that we both knew how strong I was, he'd never bother me again.

I wish I could say I was safe then. But I was about to meet a much more powerful enemy.

FRIDAY AFTERNOON

My Uncle Mike picked me up from school that afternoon. My little cousin Dana was sitting in the front middle seat of the pickup truck with us. She wouldn't stop smiling at me. It was weird.

"How was school?" my uncle asked. He stared straight ahead and waited for some kids to cross the road. He was talking to me because Dana didn't say anything. Her smile was starting to scare me. I figured she wanted something from me but was waiting for the right moment to ask.

"It was okay," I said, shrugging my shoulders. I wanted to tell him how awesome it was but that had to wait. Something was happening to me and I couldn't explain it. I had no idea how, but I was stronger than everyone else. And I had defeated Shane all by myself. "I'm just happy I made it through another week of school."

He chuckled. "When you're a kid, all you want to do is grow up." He waved at the crossing guard as we pulled onto the main highway. "But when you get to be my age, all you want to do is be a kid again." He looked over at me for the first time. "Don't be in a hurry to grow up."

I wasn't sure if he was serious or not. All I knew was I wanted to see Fox. Thanks to the agreement my mom had made with the wildlife sanctuary a while back, I got to see Fox five days a week. My uncle Mike took me there after school every day for my part time job cleaning animal cages. Sometimes I got to show visitors around the sanctuary and tell them about the animals.

"So, Joe," Dana said to me. Here it came. I couldn't wait to hear what she had been smiling about. "I haven't seen Fox in a while." She batted her eyes. "Think I could help you out today? Please, please, please, please, please, please, please, please?"

I sighed. I liked my little cousin, and she always stood up for me. She was tough as nails and didn't let anyone tell her what to do. But she liked to play with Fox and wouldn't be any help. That was a problem because there was a lot of work to do before the weekend. That's when the sanctuary was the busiest. It was a bad idea. "Maybe next time. There's too much going on right now."

She crossed her arms and stared at me with cold eyes. Her smile was gone.

"Oh, boy," my Uncle Mike said, shaking his head. "That was the wrong answer." He looked over at me and laughed. "Good luck with that."

Dana pinched my arm so hard I wanted to cry. "I'm going to help you," she assured me.

"Ouch!" I rubbed my arm. "You didn't have to do that." She was family and I'm glad she was on my side. But she didn't have to be so rough. I thought girls were supposed to be sugar and spice and everything nice.

She uncrossed her arms and said, "Sorry." She rolled her eyes and smirked. "You don't have to be a baby about it."

That was enough. I had to show her who the boss was. I did the one thing that broke her down and made her weak. I wasn't proud of it. I reached over with both hands and tickled her sides. She laughed so hard and squirmed so much that the whole truck shook. It was hilarious because she sounded like a monkey when she laughed.

"Stop, stop, stop!" Dana shouted, laughing like a crazy person. "I can't take it anymore!" So I did what any responsible kid would do. I tickled her harder.

I laughed with her until her leg jumped up and kicked the glove compartment. The compartment door busted open and a bunch of papers fell out.

"Alright, alright," my uncle said. "That's enough — both of you." He reached over and closed the door. "If I didn't know any better I'd think you were brother and sister. Geez."

I poked Dana in the side when my uncle wasn't looking. It seemed like a good idea until she pinched me again. It felt like a bee sting. I held up my hands to show her I wasn't a threat anymore. She nodded her head like she agreed to it. I wasn't sure if I could trust her so I crossed my hands over my arms to protect them.

Thirty minutes later we arrived at the wildlife sanctuary just outside of town. My heart raced in excitement when we got there. I remembered when my mom and I lived in Orlando. This was the type of excitement I felt when we went to Disney World or SeaWorld or Universal Studios.

"Have fun," my uncle said to me when the truck stopped. "Your mom already spoke with Miss Julie about the possibility of Dana helping out today." He turned his attention to Dana. "And you be on your best behavior, young lady."

I opened my door and Dana pushed me out. "Can't make any promises," she said before she jumped out behind me and closed the door. The windows were tinted but I could see my uncle shaking his head as he drove off.

"Just remember I'm in charge," I told Dana as we walked into the main office. She was seven years old and liked to boss everyone around. But not today. No sir. I was in charge.

Dana didn't see things the same way. "Keep thinking

that."

"Welcome back, Joe," Miss Julie said when she saw us. She was wearing the red shirt and white shorts she wore there every day. I didn't have to wear my uniform today because it was casual Friday. "I'm glad you could join us, Dana. There's a lot of work to do."

Dana huffed, but I reminded her that she was there to help. "It's not my job," she complained, crossing her arms. "You do it."

I couldn't wait much longer to see Fox. He was probably in the fields with his parents. I wanted to tell him what happened at school and how I beat Shane. He'd love to hear about it after what Shane and his dad had done to him.

"He's in the learning center," Miss Julie said. I wanted to see Fox before I started working, and she understood he was my best friend. "Don't take too long. There's a lot of work and I've only got you for a few hours."

I grabbed Dana's hand and headed down the hall. The learning center is where we took visitors to teach them about the animals there. We had all kinds of animals: rabbits, deer, raccoons, and even a skunk. But most importantly, we had foxes. It was our job to help raise baby animals that were abandoned. Miss Julie and other vets helped care for sick and injured animals too. They were all released once they were old enough or healthy enough to make it on their own. I had no idea why Fox would be in the learning center.

I froze when I opened the room door. Fox was standing on his hind legs at the front of the room, facing a squirrel, opossum, rabbit, and raccoon. If that wasn't weird enough, he was standing behind a podium. The brownish orange hair on his body shined brilliantly in the room's light. He held out his paws for me and Dana to wait a minute.

He spoke to the animals. "And that's the difference between a wet fart and a dry fart." He winked at me. "Class dismissed." Nine months ago, this would have been unbelievable. It was only odd now because none of the animals could understand Fox but they all wanted to be around him. He was one of a kind.

Dana ran up to Fox and hugged him. To her, he was like a walking, talking teddy bear. She never liked animals much but couldn't get enough of Fox.

"That was crazy," I told Fox. "They can't understand you. Only we can." He had gotten braver with humans ever since his performance in Las Vegas. Everyone who worked there knew he could talk. We did everything we could to hide his location from the world.

"Maybe not," Fox said. The best friend bracelet he shared with me glimmered around his wrist. I looked down at mine and smiled. It was the best birthday present I ever got. "But the fart joke was funny." I couldn't argue with him — it was hilarious. We both laughed.

Fox stumbled to the side and leaned against a table. I'd never seen him lose his balance like that.

"Are you okay?" Dana asked him.

He hit a paw against his head a few times. "The room's spinning. I just need a nap."

I was worried about him, but I had learned animals need as much as twenty hours of sleep a day. We don't see it in our pets because they change their sleeping schedules to match ours. But they do take 'cat naps' throughout the day.

"You know what we should do?" I asked Fox. I waited for him to answer with me because it was an ongoing joke with us. "We should go to China."

Fox didn't say anything. He stared at me for a minute. Then he said, "Why?"

Now he was going to play along with me. "Because they have rainbows!" But Fox didn't say anything. He looked confused.

He banged a paw against his head again. "But we have rainbows here." I waited for Fox to joke with me but it never happened. His eyes moved from side to side.

Dana grabbed my arm. "Something's wrong."

Then everything fell apart. Fox stumbled again and fell flat on his back. I raced over to him. His eyes were closed like he was asleep. "Get Miss Julie!" I shouted to Dana. "Hurry!"

She raced out of the room. I sat beside Fox and held his head in my lap. "Please be okay. Please be okay."

Miss Julie ran into the room with Dana. "Stand back," she said. "Give him some room." She bent down and ran her hands over Fox's head and body. "He's burning up."

"Do something!" Dana cried to Miss Julie. I stood and wrapped an arm around her.

Miss Julie grabbed a small flashlight from her pocket that I'd seen her use with the sick animals. She shined it into Fox's mouth and eyes. Then she turned it off and sat on the floor. "I don't understand."

"What is it?" I asked, standing behind her. "What's wrong?" I was scared to death Fox was in trouble. He had already gone through so much. He didn't deserve this.

Miss Julie turned and looked up at me. "His eyes were blue. I know they were."

I stepped around her and looked into Fox's eyes. They were gray. I'd never seen them like that. He always had bright blue eyes. What did this mean?

Miss Julie took a deep breath. "I checked his pulse and his breathing. He's okay." That was a relief. "I'm going to get some fluids in him and keep him rested for now. And I'll get his temperature down." I wasn't sure that was enough. She placed one hand on my shoulder and the other on Dana's shoulder.

"I don't know what's wrong," she admitted. "But Christopher may be able to help."

Fox was in trouble and there was nothing I could do about it. I was stronger than ever before but what good was it if I couldn't help Fox? All I could do was wait until I heard some news from the one person who could help — Christopher, a.k.a. Tater the Exterminator.

FRIDAY NIGHT

I couldn't say anything when my mom picked us up that night. My whole body was numb. Dana wouldn't stop crying. I held her close to my side while my mom hugged us both.

I almost lost Fox once. I couldn't do it again. I remembered how scared I was the first day I met him. He stared back at me with his blue eyes, stood up on his hind legs, and talked to me. I remembered how much trouble he got me into while he tried to get to our chickens. I remembered how he stood up on stage in Las Vegas and showed the world who he was. And I remembered we would always be best friends.

"He's going to be okay," my mom said when she stopped the car at home. Her voice was broken. "We have to believe that."

I wanted to believe her. I jumped out of the car and headed for the house. I froze when an orange cat with brown stripes walked in front of me, stopped, sat down, and stared up at me. It had big round yellow eyes.

"How cute," my mom said. "It's an orange tabby." She kneeled and made a clicking sound with her tongue. The cat didn't move. "Where did you come from? Don't be afraid, little guy."

Dana stood next to my side. "Is that… is it possible?" I knew what she was thinking. Maybe this cat could do the same things Fox could. Maybe it could stand up like a human and talk to us. It didn't have blue eyes, though. The cat stood on all four paws and stared up at me.

Then it did the one thing no one expected. It walked up to Dana and rubbed its sides against her legs. It purred so loud we could all hear it. It was super weird because Dana didn't like any animals except for Fox. I waited for her to kick the cat away.

Instead, she picked the orange cat up and put it over her shoulder. She patted its back and said, "I've got you, kitty cat. I'll take care of you."

My uncle pulled into the driveway in his pickup truck. He got out and stood behind Dana. "What in the world is going on?" he asked, scratching his head.

I shrugged my shoulders and kept walking toward the front door. "Welcome to the Twilight Zone." The cat was cool and all but I had to focus on Fox. Miss Julie said she'd call me if anything changed with him. I planned to wait by the phone all night.

No one talked at the dinner table later that night. My mom had made baked chicken — Fox's favorite food. I kept staring at the phone, waiting for it to ring. Dana kept looking at the door, wanting to go outside and play with the cat. My mom and uncle kept looking at each other, talking silently.

I wondered if the night would ever end. The clock on the living room wall seemed like it was broken. It felt like hours waiting for a call but only minutes had passed.

I jumped when someone knocked on the door.

"Who could that be?" my mom asked, wiping her mouth with a napkin. I didn't have any idea. She stood up and walked to the door. We all tried to see who was on the other side when she opened it. "Hello, Christopher. Come on in."

I was happy to see the exterminator who had once been a danger to Fox. I chuckled when I remembered how he thought he had big ears, but really, he had a long hotdog nose. He was wearing a green suit with a red striped tie that was way too long. We saw him every month when he sprayed pesticide around the house because my mom had prepaid him for ten years of extermination work.

"Hey, everyone," he said, waving at us. "I wanted to give you the news in person."

My heart sank. It had to be bad news if Christopher couldn't tell us over the phone. I gulped when he walked up to the dining room table. I figured there was nothing anyone could do for Fox. I was breathing so hard I had to use my mouth to get in enough air.

"He's going to be okay," Christopher assured us. He nodded at me. "He's weak, sick, and tired, but he'll make it through the night just fine."

I took a deep breath and sighed. I believed him. "What's wrong with Fox? What can we do?" My mom stood behind me and put her hands on my shoulders.

He crossed his arms. "I don't know yet. Julie contacted me because I know the best person who can help Fox now."

"Who?" my uncle asked. I forgot he was as worried about Fox as the rest of us were. He didn't approve of Fox at first, but they became friends after watching wrestling on TV together.

"I have a friend up north that may be able to help Fox," Christopher said. "He used to live around here but moved to Oklahoma a few years ago."

It didn't make any sense to me. I threw my hands up. "If the veterinarians at the sanctuary can't help, what can your friend do?"

He unfolded his arms and looked around at us. "He's not like the rest of us. We call him The Fox Whisperer."

22

I put a hand on my forehead. He was crazy. I should have known it all along. I mean, the guy called himself Tater the Exterminator because he thought he had potato ears.

"Trust me," Christopher pleaded. "He's the right person to help Fox." He nodded at me again. He wanted me to believe him. "I already called him, and he's flying here tomorrow afternoon."

I didn't know what else to say to him before he left. Tater the Exterminator had a friend named The Fox Whisperer. Dana liked an orange cat that liked her back. And I was just a normal kid that was stronger than everyone else now. I didn't think my life could get any weirder. But it did.

SATURDAY MORNING

I didn't get any sleep the night before. I had a hard time standing up behind our table at the farmers market. I argued with my mom that I needed to check on Fox and couldn't come today. She told me that he was in good hands and there was nothing we could do until the Fox Whisperer got there. And this would keep me busy and distracted. I was mad about it but there I was, selling eggs with her like I did every Saturday.

"Brave enough to try an egg today?" my mom yelled over to Mr. Jim Bob at the fruit and vegetable table next to us. I always saw him with that straw hat on and wondered if it was glued to his head. He wore a clean pair of overalls. I wondered if he owned any short pants or tank tops.

"Not on your life," he replied in his strong country accent. I didn't expect him to after he ate Old Nelly's rotten eggs. I missed that chicken. I would never forget she said I was chosen. I wished I knew what I was chosen for.

"Excuse me," a man I had never seen before said when he walked up to our table. He had light brown skin that reminded me of the Jet Li movies I used to watch with my dad. He wore a black suit without a tie. And there were two bigger men like him standing behind him like bodyguards. "How much are the eggs?" He picked one up and smelled it.

My mom didn't waste any time going into her sales pitch about how our chickens were farm raised. She said our eggs tasted better than store bought eggs. I didn't know if that was true or not. Eggs always tasted the same to me after they were scrambled. "It's six dollars for half a dozen eggs."

The man snapped his fingers. One of the big guys behind him handed him some money.

"I haven't seen you before," my mom told him. We knew everyone in that town after being there for almost a year. "You're not from around here, are you?" She smiled and took his money.

He didn't smile back. "I'm here on business from China." I wished Fox was there right then. I remembered how he liked to stand behind people and scare them by raising his paws and shouting, "Chinese sneak attack!"

The man bowed and said, "You may call me Chen."

"Nice to meet you, Chen," my mom said. "My name is Julie." She pulled me close to her side. "And this is my son, Jonah."

I wished my mom would stop calling me that. "Please call me Joe," I told him.

He nodded and reached a hand out to shake mine. I froze when his hand touched my skin. It was as cold as ice. I'm not kidding. I don't remember touching anything that cold in my entire life. Goose bumps shot up all over my body. He stared at me with angry eyes. I stepped back. I had to get away from him.

"China," my mom said. "That sounds exciting. I hope we can go there one day." I hoped I never had to go there. I hoped I never had to see this man again.

I was relieved when Mr. Hunter stepped up to our table. I didn't think I'd be so happy to see the old man with a bald head and bushy eyebrows. "Hey, Joe. Is everything okay?" He looked over at Mr. Chen and the two big guys with him.

I was scared of Mr. Chen. How could I let Mr. Hunter know that? I should have blinked hard three times. But I didn't have to.

Mr. Chen snapped his fingers again. The big guys behind him moved to the side so he could turn around. "I need to go now."

My mom held up a hand. "Don't forget your eggs."

He shook his head and said, "Keep them." He looked straight at me and said something that made me swallow hard. "I'll see you soon, Joe." He turned and marched off with the two big guys following him.

I was glad Mr. Hunter showed up when he did. He had saved me more than once. Like when he bought all my chocolate. It seemed so long ago that I had tried to earn enough money to help save my great-grandma's house.

"What time is it?" Mrs. Hunter said when she joined her husband on the other side of the table. She smiled at my mom and said, "Hello, dear." She smiled at me too. "Hi, Joe." Me and my mom both smiled back at her and said our hellos.

"Look at that," Mr. Hunter said, holding his wrist up in the air and pointing at his watch. "It's my favorite time of day." He lowered his wrist and smirked at me. "Nap time."

I laughed. I don't think I've taken a nap since I was four years old.

"Laugh all you want," he said, crossing his arms. "While you're mowing the lawn or doing chores, I'll be dreaming about lying on the beach and eating tacos."

Mrs. Hunter frowned and shook her head. "Unfortunately, he's not kidding." She jabbed an elbow into his side. "That's what happens when you become an old fart."

My mom reached for her pocket and pulled her phone out. She put it to her ear. "Hello?" she said, turning from all of us so we could keep talking. I liked the Hunters but I had to know if that was Christopher on the phone. He said he'd call as soon as his friend got into town.

"Uh huh," my mom said into the phone. "Yes. Okay." I hated listening to one side of a conversation. I could only guess what the other person was saying. "We'll be right there." She closed her phone and put it back into her pocket.

She was taking too long to tell me what was going on. "It was him, wasn't it?" I hoped it was so he could help Fox.

She placed a sign on the table that said FREE EGGS. Then she nodded and said, "Yes. Let's go." I walked away without looking back. "Sorry about this," my mom said to the Hunters. "We'll catch up later."

Mr. Hunter threw his hands up. "Where are you going so fast? What about the eggs?"

My mom raced behind me towards the parking lot. "Keep the eggs!" she yelled to the Hunters. "They're on the house!"

"I never turn down a free meal!" Mr. Hunter shouted back, rubbing his hands together. "Unless it's broccoli! I hate broccoli!

SATURDAY AFTERNOON

I wasn't sure what to say when the Fox Whisperer asked me questions at the sanctuary. His name was Elan, which he explained means 'friendly'. He had darker skin than mine, like Chen's. Miss Julie told me that he was an American Indian. I had seen a lot of movies with my dad that had cowboys and Indians in them. But the Fox Whisperer didn't look like any of them. He wore jeans and tennis shoes, had an awesome haircut, and never stopped smiling.

"Were his eyes always bright blue before?" Elan asked me. I looked over at Fox. He was stretched out and asleep with a blanket over him on a table to keep him comfort-table. I wondered how much Miss Julie had told Elan. She stood by his side and nodded at me.

"For as long as I've known him," I admitted. I had no idea if his eyes were bright blue before that. I never thought about it.

"How did you first meet him?" Elan pressed. I wasn't sure how much information to give him. Fox was sick and the Fox Whisperer was supposed to help him. That was his job, right?

"None of that's important," my mom said. She stood by my side. She could read my mind. We were both afraid Fox's abilities to walk and talk would be discovered.

"It's okay," Miss Julie said to us. "Elan's seen the video. He knows what Fox can do." I wished the video Shane had recorded never existed. It was the only reason Fox was there in the first place.

My mom said it was okay to tell Elan everything. "I met him at our chicken coop last year," I told Elan. I remembered how Fox had stared at me and smiled.

"Is that far from here?" Elan asked. I wasn't sure why that would make any difference.

"It's about thirty miles," my mom said. "In Andalusia."

Elan put a hand on his chin and paced around the room. He kept looking over at Fox. "I've been searching for a long time." What did he mean? What was he searching for? He was making me nervous the same way Dana did when she smiled at me.

"What are you talking about?" Miss Julie asked. She was checking Fox's eyes and throat again while he was asleep. His tongue was hanging out of the side of his mouth with slobber all over it.

Elan stopped pacing the room and looked around at us. "There were eight Indian tribes here in Alabama before we were forced to leave." He shook his head like he was disappointed. "Now there's only one."

I didn't understand. Why would anyone make them leave? I looked up at my mom. "That's not fair. Why did this happen?"

He smiled at me. "It was in the 1800s — long before you were born. The United States was young, like you." He stepped in front of me and put a hand on my shoulder. "You are pure and strong, Joe. Have your eyes always been blue?"

What was he talking about? I had brown eyes. He pulled a small mirror out of his pocket, just like the mirror Miss Julie had to check the animals with. He held it in front of my eyes. They were bright blue!

"Tell me something, Joe..." He winked at me. "Have you noticed anything different? Are you faster, stronger, or smarter than you were before?"

I gulped. Months ago, I had almost beaten Shane at an arm wrestling contest. And yesterday I did more pull-ups than anyone else. And come to think of it, I was the only person in my sixth-grade classes to get straight A's — I had never done that before. I didn't want to tell Elan any of that because I was afraid I'd become a science project.

Elan bent down and looked into my eyes. "It's okay. You were chosen."

Goosebumps ran down my arms. I remembered Old Nelly saying those exact words to me in the chicken coop. I was stronger and smarter than I had ever been before. But why me? Why was I so special?

Elan stood back up and walked over to Fox. He stroked Fox's head. "There was one tribe you won't find any records of. I heard stories about them my entire childhood." His eyes became blank like he was remembering something. "They called themselves The Talking Dragons. They believed humans and animals could work together."

My mom held me close. "Is my son going to be okay? You have to do something!" She sounded hysterical, like she was about to cry.

Elan smiled at her. "He's going to be better than okay. There's nothing to worry about."

My mom held me tighter. "How can you say that?" she shouted. "Look at what's happening to Fox!"

Miss Julie put her hands up in front of her. "We all need to calm down. Elan didn't come here because he had to. He just came to help."

My mom took a deep breath and stared at Elan. "What do we do?"

Elan nodded. "Fox's abilities come from the land he was on. The land owned by The Talking Dragons." He smiled at me again. He had a way of making me feel safe and comfortable. "Fox must go back to the land he was chosen by."

My mom let go of me and crossed her arms. "What about my son?"

Elan flashed his magic smile. "The land chooses those who are pure of heart. Joe is more special than you can ever imagine."

I didn't know if any of what Elan said was true. I hoped he could help make Fox better. It didn't matter if I was stronger or smarter if I couldn't share it with my best friend. I was about to find out for sure.

SATURDAY NIGHT

I looked at the outhouse as we walked past it. My mom, Miss Julie, and Elan were with me. Fox was in Elan's arms, wrapped in a blanket. My uncle and Dana waited for us in the backyard by the chicken coop.

I remembered the day I opened the outhouse door for the first time. I ran for my life when a grasshopper jumped out and surprised me. Dana and Fox had walked in circles, flapping their arms, making chicken sounds, and laughing at me. I was embarrassed that day but I wished I could get it back.

Dana ran up to Elan and Fox. "Is he going to be okay?" she asked, walking backwards while facing them. She rubbed Fox's head. He was still asleep.

"We'll know soon," Elan promised. He turned to me. "Where did you meet him, Joe? Around here?"

I pictured Fox's bright blues looking back at me when I stepped out of the chicken coop nine months ago. "Yes." I pointed at the spot Fox had stood on his hind legs and asked me where my collar was.

Elan laid Fox on the ground and took the blanket off him. Fox looked so young and healthy with his brownish orange hair, white chest and tail, and black paws. I didn't understand how he could be sick. "The land will decide what happens next," Elan said, stepping away from Fox.

What did he mean? I thought all we had to do was take Fox there and everything would be better. "You said this would help him." I tried not to cry. "It has to work."

"The land will decide," Elan repeated. He smiled at me again but I could tell he was concerned. I wasn't sure he believed anything he told us about the land and The Talking Dragon tribe. He made everything up. He was another crazy person like Tater the Exterminator. I should have known better than to trust either of them.

"Maybe we should dance around him and chant like the Indians do," Dana said. I shook my head. My mom must have told her that Elan was an American Indian.

"That's not going to help," Elan told her. He wasn't smiling anymore.

The night got darker and darker. My legs were hurting from standing for so long, so I sat down in the grass. This was a waste of time. There had to be another way to help Fox. I wanted to grab Fox and take him to my room. But that wouldn't help.

Dana sat next to me. "He's going to be okay, right?" she asked. There were tears in her eyes. She didn't think this was going to work either. "Hey, what's going on with your eyes?"

I turned away from her. "Nothing."

She grabbed my head and turned it toward hers.

"They're blue, just like Fox's." She probably thought I was a freak. "You're so lucky."

I didn't feel lucky. I needed to steer the attention away from me. "Where's your cat?"

Dana shrugged. "I haven't seen him since last night. He was a stray cat." Her eyes lit up and she laughed. "I've got a name for him if he comes back." Her shoulders shook every time she laughed.

"Spit it out," I told her. "What is it?"

She looked at me with serious eyes. "Peanut Butter Jelly."

I chuckled. "What? Why?"

She scooted in close. "Any time I spend with him… I can call it Peanut Butter Jelly time!"

We both laughed and started singing a song we heard on the internet, *"It's peanut butter jelly time, peanut butter jelly time…"*

I froze when I saw one of Fox's paws move. He was waking up. I stood and brushed my pants off. Dana bumped into me when she stood up too. My mom, uncle, Miss Julie, and Elan were on the other side of Fox. We all stared at him to see what would happen next.

It was slow. Fox stretched his legs out and yawned. His ears perked up. His eyes were still closed. My heart was beating fast. Did it work? Was he better?

Fox stood on all four paws, smiled, and opened his eyes. They were bright blue! He rose slowly on his two hind legs, raised a paw into the air, and said something that let me know everything was okay.

"My name is Mr. Awesome Muscles!"

I laughed and gave him a high five. Dana tackled him when she hugged him. My mom and Miss Julie both shook Elan's hand. He wasn't crazy after all.

Elan walked over to me and gave me a fist pump. "Trust the land." I nodded. I wasn't sure what the land had chosen me for, but it had saved Fox.

As I watched everyone hug Fox and talk with him, one realization hit me: he could never leave this land again. This is what gave him the power to walk and talk. It protected him. And without it, he would be sick. We couldn't be sure what would happen to him if he went away again. He couldn't go back to the sanctuary. I didn't know how to tell him that he may never see his parents again.

SUNDAY MORNING

I woke up because the sun was shining through my bedroom window and right into my eyes. I scooted further down the bed so the light wouldn't make me blind. That was better. A couple of birds were chirping outside. It made me smile.

Fox was asleep in the blanket den I had made for him months ago. I had never taken it down because I hoped he would return one day. I would have slept next to him on the floor but he was restless and kept kicking me in the side. And his paws were like ice cubes when they touched my back.

I sat up and lifted the blanket closest to my bed. Fox was laying in the middle of the den on his stomach with all four hairy legs straight out like an airplane. He was facedown with his tongue sticking out. There was slobber all over my favorite pillow. Yes, I let him sleep on my favorite pillow. He could keep it now. Yuck!

I laid back down and thought about how perfect everything was. Fox was back with us and not in any more danger. He could stay there forever.

My mom threw my bedroom door open and rushed into my room. "Jonah! Get up right now." Her hands were in the air. "Why are you still in bed?"

I didn't know why she was so upset. I had plenty of time to get ready for Sunday School and church. My alarm clock hadn't gone off yet. I sat up and blocked the sun from my eyes. I looked over at my clock on the table next my bed.

Only, it wasn't there! Oh, no. Where was my clock? I

jumped out of bed and said, "Sorry."

My mom had her arms crossed and was tapping a foot on the floor. She didn't like being late for anything. "Breakfast is on the kitchen table. Hurry up." She stormed out of the room, shaking her head.

I lifted the den blankets and yelled at Fox to wake up. He grabbed a sheet and pulled it up over his head. And that's when I saw it. My alarm clock was crushed and broken into pieces by Fox's back paws.

I snatched the sheet away from Fox. He crossed his legs and paws, and shivered. "What is this?" I yelled at him. "What did you do to my clock?" It looked like he had smashed it with a hammer. My mom was mad at me because of what Fox had done. Some things never change.

He yawned and looked at the broken pieces. "Oh, that." He stretched his legs and stared at me. "You're not gonna believe this." I couldn't wait to hear it.

"So here I was," Fox continued, "sleeping nice and quietly, minding my own business." He sat up. "All of the sudden I heard screaming by your bed." His eyes got big. He pointed to the broken alarm clock. "It was jumping around like a bunny rabbit on five cups of coffee."

I couldn't help but laugh. Bunny rabbits don't drink coffee. At least I don't think they do.

"I pounced on the little monster," Fox said. "I defeated it." He stood on his two hind legs. I could tell he was proud of himself because he had saved me. "No thanks needed. Maybe some chicken, but that's all."

I threw on a pair of shorts and a tee-shirt. "Come with me," I told Fox, heading for the kitchen. I couldn't be mad at him. He still had a lot to learn. Now he was back, we had all the time in the world for that.

"Glad you could make it," my mom said when we walked into the kitchen. "Eat your breakfast. Then wash up and get dressed for church." Her face was red. We had missed Sunday School. "There's no excuse," she muttered. "There's really no excuse."

I felt bad but it wasn't my fault. "Fox ate my alarm clock," I told her. I sat down at the table, grabbed the plate with my omelet and sipped on a glass of milk.

Fox sat across from me with his own omelet. "Traitor," he whispered.

My mom stepped behind Fox and rubbed his head. "You poor thing," she said to him. "You must be starving. You were gone for months and they didn't feed you properly." She nodded her head like she fixed something. "I'll make sure you always have chicken."

Fox ate the omelet with a big smile on his face. He winked at me.

I bit into my omelet and spit it out. It didn't taste anything like the eggs we normally ate. "What is this?" I asked my mom. "What did you put in my egg?" Was she trying to poison me?

She waved a hand like she was insulted by what I said. "It's a chicken omelet. It has chicken, onions, and banana peppers." Banana peppers? Who ever heard of that? "Oh, and I added a hint of cayenne and cheese."

Fox burped when he finished his omelet. "I like it." He looked at mine. "Are you gonna eat that?" I shook my head and pushed my plate across the table to him. Before he sunk his teeth into my omelet, he had the nerve to say to me, "Now that you have some free time, you can make me another chicken omelet."

My mom laughed with him. It wasn't funny. Fox wasn't the one who was starving. I was!

"Hey, Fox!" Dana shouted when she and my uncle walked into the house. She raced into the kitchen and kissed his cheek.

"We can't miss the wrestling match today," my uncle said to Fox from behind me. "World Championship. Mr. Awesome Muscles versus King Thunderbutt." He sounded super excited.

I didn't mind that Fox got so much attention, but I felt invisible. "I'm right here," I complained to them. "In case anyone cares."

My uncle squeezed my shoulders. Dana rolled her eyes at me. "Hey, Joe," she said, "you've got egg on your face." I wiped my face as fast as I could. There was nothing there. Dana and Fox laughed.

I had to laugh with them. "You got me." I let them talk all they wanted to while I got up to get ready for church. Dana would go with me and my mom. My uncle and Fox would stay there to watch the men in underwear fight on TV. I looked back at them and smiled. It was awesome seeing them together like this. We weren't all born from the same blood, but we were all family.

LATER SUNDAY MORNING

I was officially a Back Row Baptist. Dana and Melissa sat there with me every Sunday morning now. It gave us a chance to talk without being disturbed. Today I needed to figure out what to do with Fox. He was healthy again but he couldn't go back to the sanctuary.

Melissa was in her blue Sunday dress with polka dots. Dana wore a nice white dress. I wore slacks and a buttoned down white shirt. I wore a black tie with it — not the kind most guys wore. Mine was a clip on that snapped onto my shirt in a flash. The regular ties were like rope you wrap around your neck. No thanks!

I told Melissa about everything that had happened the night before. I had promised to be honest with her. And I needed her opinion. I would have asked Dana, but every time I looked at her, I started singing *"It's peanut butter jelly time"* in my head.

Before I could say anything, the one person I never expected to see there tapped me on the shoulder.

I turned around and looked up at my sworn enemy. It was Shane. He was smiling at me. What was he doing there? That was my one place to be surrounded by family and friends. It was the only place I could think clearly and feel safe. And now he was going to ruin it.

"Joe," he said, looking at me with a straight face. I was confused. He had always called me Jonah. "I'm sorry. For everything." I froze. I didn't believe him, and I had no idea how to respond.

His dad grabbed him and led him towards the front of the church. I couldn't breathe. Mr. Connors and Shane were the ones who had put Fox in so much danger. They had no right to be there! They couldn't be trusted. My blood was boiling.

"Calm down, Joe," Melissa said, grabbing my hand. "Breathe. It's going to be okay." I wanted to believe her. But I was disgusted. I was breathing so hard that my chest hurt.

Dana scooted forward and put her hands together. "We should pray for Shane," she encouraged me. She closed her eyes. "Dear Lord, please let Shane trip over his feet and fall on his face. Amen." I couldn't help but say "amen" with her.

"Hey, Joe!" I jumped when Mr. Hunter stepped into my row and said, "Be sure to thank your mom for the eggs." I nodded at him before his wife grabbed him and pulled him away.

The church organist played the same song she did every Sunday. The service was about to start. From his seat up front, Shane turned and stared at me. I couldn't have been more uncomfortable.

The man in front of me stretched his arm over the pew and turned his head toward me. It was the man from China — Mr. Chen! His eyes were cold. "Hello, Joe. It's good to see you again." It wasn't good to see him. The two bodyguards he had with him at the farmers market were sitting on either side of him. Shane didn't matter anymore. This man made me feel more afraid than anyone else.

"Brothers and sisters," the pastor said to the congregation. "God is good." Several voices said amen. "Whatever you're afraid of today, give it to God." I swear he was looking right at me. "Fear not, my child. I am with you always."

I wanted to believe that more than anything, but I was surrounded by serpents. The people who tried to destroy me and Fox were only a few pews away. And the man who made me shake in fear was right in front of me. I thought about sneaking out and waiting for my mom in the car. With the doors locked.

"Love your enemies and pray for those who persecute you," the preacher continued. Dana had already prayed for Shane. That was good enough for me. The service was taking forever and I thought it would never end.

But then the organist played the same song again. It was time to disappear. "We need to get out of here, right now," I whispered to Dana. I grabbed Melissa's hand and pulled her along as Dana shouted for people to get out of the way.

Before we were out of the aisle, I noticed Mr. Chen and his bodyguards hadn't moved an inch. He was perfectly happy to sit there until everyone else left. What did this mean? Was I crazy? I had to be. Why would this man be any danger to me?

He turned and faced me again. "See you soon, Joe." He gave me a curt wave and faced the front again.

"Joe, wait!" Shane shouted from the front of the church. His dad held him back. "I have to talk to you!"

I wasn't going to fall for any of his tricks. He had pushed me down at school and kicked me at my birthday party. There was no telling what he would do to me in the church. He was despicable.

I pushed through the crowd until we were in the foyer again. The preacher stopped me. How did he get back there? He was just up front, preaching and singing.

"Is everything okay, Joe?" he asked me.

I didn't want to lie to him. "I thought so. But I don't know anymore." I had to keep moving. There wasn't any time to explain.

He put a hand on my shoulder. "We may not always have the answers but we can always have faith. Sometimes we have to get out of our own way to see things clearly."

"Joe, wait!" Shane shouted from somewhere in the crowd.

I thanked the preacher and rushed out with Dana and Melissa. With any luck, my mom would meet us by the car and get us out of there. Everything was supposed to be better. Why did I feel like it was a lot worse? I wanted to get home and talk to my best friend.

I'm glad I got the chance to before I lost him forever.

SUNDAY AFTERNOON

I never expected what I found when I walked into my house. It horrified me. "What in the world?"

Fox was sitting at a princess table with four teacups on it. He motioned for all of us to join him for a teacup party. Dana had tried for years to get me to play with her but I refused to do it.

"Out of the way," Dana said, shoving me to the side. She and Melissa joined Fox at the table. They pretended to pour drinks and sip on them. They talked in English accents. I won't lie — it looked fun. But I had to keep my cool image.

My uncle looked at me from the couch. He was watching wrestling. He shrugged his shoulders. "I did what I could."

"A fox has to do what a fox has to do," Fox explained. "I was promised a chicken party if I did this first." He pretended to pour himself another cup of tea and said, "Cheers!"

My mom walked in and closed the door behind her. She smiled at Dana, Melissa, and Fox. "How cute! I'm gonna have to get my camera." There was no chance in the world you'd find me sitting at the table. "Joe," she said to me, "come join me and Uncle Mike on the couch first. We need to talk."

That made me feel proud. I was asked to join the secret society of adults. The kids could play games at the princess table while the adults talked on the couch. How awesome is that?

My mom grabbed the remote from my uncle and Turned the TV off. He grunted. "We need a plan," she said when we were on the couch. "What are we going to do with Fox?"

As far as I was concerned, Fox could stay with us forever. It wasn't legal for us to keep him, but no one had to know. "He still has the den I made for him. He knows all of us and we love him. He's our family."

My uncle nodded his agreement and tried to grab the remote from my mom. She slapped his hand away.

"I was thinking something else," my mom said.

My uncle rubbed his forehead. "Is that something else going to take more than three minutes?" She crossed her arms and stared at him. "I was just asking," my uncle said with his hands up for protection.

She shook her head and sighed. "I was thinking Fox's parents are getting better and they're going to be released soon." I hadn't thought of that. None of the animals were meant to stay at the sanctuary forever. "What if we can work it out so they're released back where they came from?"

I knew what she meant. They had come from somewhere around there, deep in the woods. Fox had said he wandered for days until he found the chicken coop. Their home couldn't be far from there.

"You're right," I told her. "That's the best idea ever. That way, Fox will always be close by." She smiled and messed up my hair.

I wanted to tell Fox the good news but someone knocked on the door. "I'll get it," I told everyone. I was in such a good mood that nothing could bring me down. I'd get to keep seeing my best friend and he'd stay united with his parents forever.

Time stopped when I opened the door. I was wrong thinking that nothing could bring me down. Things couldn't get any worse.

"Hello, Joe," Mr. Chen said to me from the doorstep. His bodyguards were behind him. He was wearing a pair of mirrored sunglasses. He took the glasses off and said, "Give us the fox."

All at once I remembered when we came home from Las Vegas. The house had been torn apart. The furniture was ripped to shreds. The pictures and TV were smashed. And someone had painted the words GIVE US THE FOX on the wall above the door.

These men were dangerous. I reached for the door to slam it shut. But Chen kept it open with his hands and kicked it down. He shoved me to the floor and marched right past me with his henchmen behind him.

"Where is he?" Chen shouted into the room. Then he saw Fox sitting at the princess table with a teacup in his hands. Chen smirked.

My mom and uncle jumped up from the couch and looked at the three men. I figured they were trying to determine if they could stop them.

Chen glared at them and snapped his fingers. One of his henchmen walked over to the couch and stood in front of my mom and uncle, daring them to try and stop him.

"If you hurt these children," my mom hissed, "I will hunt you down. You'll be sorry you ever walked into this house."

Chen laughed and said, "Promises, promises." He returned his attention to Fox. "I've been looking for you a long time. You have no idea how important you are." He snapped his fingers again.

His second henchman headed for the princess table where Dana, Melissa, and Fox were. Melissa shrieked. Dana stood up. "Stay away from him!" she yelled.

The henchman pushed her back into her seat. I got up to protect her, but Chen wagged a finger at me to let me know there was nothing I could do.

But maybe there was. I was chosen for something. I was stronger and smarter than I had ever been before. This was why. The land had chosen me to protect everyone.

"Stop," Fox said. "Just stop." He stood on his hind legs and put his paws out. "No one has to get hurt." He looked at me and nodded. "We knew it wasn't safe for me to stay here." He looked up at Chen. "Just take me. Do whatever you have to. Leave them out of it."

He was sacrificing himself. I had no idea what these men wanted with him but they proved they were dangerous. There's no way Fox could go with them.

Chen laughed again. "The fox is wise." He took two steps toward the table. "My employers in China are very interested in you."

The henchman grabbed Fox and held his legs together so he couldn't move. Melissa had a hand over her mouth.

"They're going to take you apart, piece by piece," Chen continued. "Like a clock. They're going to find out what makes you tick." I wasn't going to allow that to happen. I balled my fists and prepared to attack. But I never got the chance.

The back door in the kitchen barreled open and slammed against the wall. "Who else is here?" Chen asked. No one answered because no one else was supposed to be there. We had no idea who it was. Chen snapped his fingers. The henchman who was standing in front of the couch headed for the kitchen.

He didn't have to. The chubby man with a huge forehead and a hotdog nose stepped into the room. It was Tater the Exterminator!

"Everything's going to be okay!" Tater shouted. He was carrying a big bottle of pesticide and waving the spray stick around. "I got all the ants, roaches, and termites for miles!" He wouldn't stop his crazy laugh with his tongue hanging out.

"Who are you?" Chen shouted.

Tater kept laughing. "You don't know who I am? They know me around these parts! I'm Tater the Exterminator!"

Chen nodded at his henchman. "Take him down." The man marched straight for Tater. I thought for sure he was going to hurt him. I was wrong.

Tater whipped his spray stick right in front of the man's face and sprayed the pesticide full force. The man screamed and scratched at his eyes.

One down.

"Fox!" I yelled. The second henchman turned to face me. Fox was locked in his arms. He could only move his head and tail. "His arms look like chicken legs." I pointed at the man.

Fox didn't do anything at first but then his eyes lit up. He opened his mouth wide and used his razor-sharp teeth to chomp on the man's arm. The henchman screamed and threw Fox down.

"Enough!" Chen yelled. "You can't stop this!"

The front door busted open again. Three men in uniforms pointed guns inside. "FBI!" one of them shouted. "Nobody move!"

Chen tried to run for the back door, but Dana stuck her foot out and tripped him. I cringed when his face hit the floor like a brick. Dana shook her head at him. "Don't ever disturb my tea party again. I'm a princess."

It took a few minutes but the FBI agents handcuffed Chen and his henchmen and took them away. One stayed behind to ask us questions. Melissa ran over to me and asked if I was okay. I was, but I wished I could have done more. I didn't use any of my gifts. But there was one thing I had to do.

"I need to tell you something," I said to Melissa. "We've been friends for a while." My stomach felt like it was doing belly flops on the kitchen floor. "I like you — a lot."

"That's sweet," she said. "I like you a lot too." She blushed and giggled.

I couldn't say anything else when Shane walked into my house. What was he doing there? Had he followed me? Why couldn't he leave me alone?

"Look us up in a few years," the FBI agent said to Shane on his way out. "We can use men like you. You did a good thing here."

What was the agent talking about? Mr. Hunter walked in and patted Shane on the shoulder. "Thank you, son."

"What's going on?" I asked when they walked up to me and Melissa. Why was everyone thanking my sworn enemy?

"I watch a lot of crime shows," Shane said. "I had a lot of free time after my dad and I were arrested in Las Vegas." I didn't care about his personal life. He probably watched crime shows so he knew how to commit crime.

"When we were in church," Shane continued, "I recognized the man in front of you. He's the most wanted man in America."

I gulped. The most wanted man in America had been following me and attacked my family? I didn't feel good at all.

"I saw him watching you," Shane said. "I knew you were in trouble." He shook his head. "I tried to get your attention, but I don't think you heard me."

I remembered him shouting my name in the church. I realized he wasn't staring at me. He was keeping an eye on Chen.

"Your friend's a real hero," Mr. Hunter said. He shook Shane's hand. "He told me everything after he couldn't get your attention in church. Honestly, I thought he was a crazy kid." He laughed. "He insisted we call the police. The rest is history."

Dana joined us. "That doesn't explain Tater being here."

Mr. Hunter and Shane both shrugged. No one knew why Tater showed up when he did, but we were sure glad he did.

"I was spraying your garden out back, like I do every third Sunday," Tater said to my mom and uncle. "I heard those bad men barge into your house. I looked through the window and saw you were in trouble." He pounded his fists. "I wasn't gonna let them hurt my friends."

My mom hugged him. "I always had a good feeling about you, Christopher."

I searched the room for Fox. He liked to be the center of attention but I didn't hear anything from him. He was sitting at the princess table, staring at the teacups.

I sat across from him. "Hey, buddy. Are you okay?"

He looked at me but didn't smile like he usually did. "I can't do this anymore. I put you in danger."

I had good news for him. I told him what I had discussed with my mom and uncle. He could go back to his old home with his parents. It had to be nearby. And he could see us whenever he wanted to.

I expected him to be thrilled. He wasn't. "I want my old life back," he begged.

"I'm confused," I told him. "I just said you can have it."

Fox sighed. "You don't understand. As long as I can walk and talk, you'll always be in danger."

I took a deep breath. He was talking about returning to

the wild and being the way he used to be. I couldn't accept that. He was my best friend. I would lose him forever if he was nothing more than a wild animal. It didn't make any difference anyways. He'd be sick without his powers.

"None of this is your fault," I assured him. "I'm sorry, but there's not a way to go back."

"Actually," someone said from behind me, "there may be a way." I turned and looked up to see the American Indian, Elan smiling at me with a laptop in his hands. "Christopher called me and said it was an emergency. It's time for me to tell you everything."

Everyone gathered around the table. Elan looked at the group. "I haven't been completely honest with you." I knew it! He made everything up about the Talking Dragon Tribe and the land having power.

"You lied?" my mom asked. "Why?"

He shook his head. "I never lied." He focused on Fox. "I have been searching for you and this land my entire life. I am the last tribal member of the Talking Dragons."

My head wouldn't stop spinning. I lived on historic American Indian land that no one else knew about. And the last member of that tribe stood in front of me. It should have been a dream come true.

SUNDAY NIGHT

My stomach twisted inside and out as we walked past the outhouse again. We were about to say goodbye to Fox forever.

I was surrounded by so many people that Fox had touched. It wasn't just my mom, uncle, Dana, and Melissa. There was also Elan, Miss Julie, Tater, and Mr. Hunter. Ms. Julie had brought Fox's parents. Shane lurked behind everyone like he was ashamed. This was like going to a funeral.

We stopped in front of the chicken coop, where this all started. It was bittersweet. I wanted the best for Fox. But I didn't want to lose him.

"Form a circle around Fox," Elan said. Fox's parents stood on either side of him.

Melissa grabbed my hand and squeezed it. I wrapped my other arm around Dana's shoulders. She was crying.

"So," Dana said through tears, "now are we supposed to dance or chant something?" She tried to laugh but it turned into a cough.

"I know you're all worried," Elan said. "And I can't lie. I've never done this before." He smiled wide at us to make us feel calm. "But we're doing this so Fox can live his life the way it was meant to be. It's what he wants."

My mom and uncle were on the other side of the circle. They both wiped away tears. My uncle and Fox were wrestling buddies. My mom treated Fox like he was one of her own children.

Shane and Mr. Hunter were on my right. Shane

had always been my enemy and had helped kidnap Fox to destroy me. But something had changed in him. He had helped save Fox. It was weird to think we might be friends one day. Mr. Hunter didn't know Fox very well, but he had always supported me.

Christopher and Miss Julie were on my left. They had proven to be the most valuable to Fox. They helped him and his parents. I had misjudged Christopher at first. I laughed when I remembered he thought he had potato ears, when he really had a hotdog nose.

"You'll want to say your goodbyes to Fox," Elan said. "Once he returns to his natural state, he may not remember any of this or any of us."

I waited for everyone else to hug Fox and tell him goodbye. There were a lot of tears. It was hard to stand there and watch. I tried to swallow but I couldn't. My throat wouldn't move.

"I'm gonna miss you," Dana said to Fox, with tears in her eyes. "Thanks for the tea party. No one else ever did that for me." She bent down and hugged him.

He winked at her. "I hope you don't think I forgot." She shrugged. "You owe me a chicken party." They laughed and waved goodbye.

My mom was the last person to speak with Fox before me. "You're a good fox," she said. "No matter what happens, always remember we love you."

Fox hugged her leg. "You're a second mom to me. Thank you, Mom." My mom held her chest when she walked away. I thought she was going to fall over.

And then Fox was standing alone in the center. It was my turn to say goodbye. I forced my legs to move toward him. They felt like cement.

We faced each other but didn't say anything for the longest time. I was cold and sweating. My heart wouldn't stop racing. I couldn't breathe. I wanted to beg him to stay.

"You know what we should do?" Fox asked.

"We should go to China," I replied, trying not to smile.

Fox shook his head. "No, we shouldn't. Not after today." We both burst out laughing. He was right. He raised his paws into the air and said, "Chinese sneak attack!"

We both fell on the ground laughing. Just like the old days. "Thank you for everything," Fox said. "I mean it."

I stood up with him and hugged him. "Thank you for being my friend." I held out my wrist with the best friend bracelet he had gotten me for my birthday. He held out his. "Best friends forever," we said together.

I stepped out of the circle. Fox's parents stood by his side again. He was doing the right thing. He was a good fox.

We all clasped hands when Elan spoke in a language we had never heard. I guessed it was the language of his ancestors, The Talking Dragons. I didn't take my eyes off Fox. I had to see if anything changed about him.

Nothing happened until a few minutes later. I watched Fox's eyes change from blue to brown.

Elan stopped talking. He told us to give Fox some room because he might not recognize us and become scared. We broke the circle and gathered in one group. Fox looked at us like he was confused. Like he was trapped. His wide eyes seemed afraid of us.

"Fox!" I called out. "It's me, Joe. Remember?"

Fox stared at me, then he turned and ran off into the woods. His parents followed him. He was afraid of me. He didn't recognize me. It was like I never existed to him. I covered my eyes and cried more than I ever had before.

My mom held me and kept saying, "Shhhh. It's going to be okay." I wished I could believe her. I heard Dana crying in my uncle's arms. That made me cry harder.

A few minutes passed. Or maybe hours. Melissa patted me on the arm. "Joe. Look."

I turned and followed her gaze. Fox was walking slowly out of the woods. Everyone backed away to let me stand in the open all by myself.

As Fox got closer, he inched slower and slower on his four legs. I wasn't sure he recognized me, but he sensed we had a connection.

I stayed still as he came closer and sniffed my shoes and pants. He looked skittish, like he would run if I moved even a little. He stopped sniffing when he saw the bracelet on my wrist.

He looked back and forth from his bracelet to mine. He was remembering. "Best friends forever," I whispered. He licked my hand, bowed his head, then turned and ran back into the woods.

He remembered me! Not completely, but our bond would never be broken.

"Do you think we'll ever see him again?" Dana asked when she joined me. Melissa was with her.

"I hope so," I told her, smiling.

The adults and Shane were talking behind us. We were all sad and excited. Fox would always be a part of our lives.

"Look!" Dana shouted. The stray orange tabby walked around her legs and purred. "It's Peanut Butter Jelly!"

"That cat's been out here all night," Melissa said. "I saw him by the chicken coop earlier. He stared at Fox the whole time he was talking to us." She faced Dana. "Why would you call him Peanut Butter Jelly?"

Dana and I laughed and started singing *"It's peanut butter jelly time, peanut butter jelly time…"*

The orange tabby meowed while we sang. I think it wanted us to stop. It walked away from us and towards the woods. And then it did the one thing I never expected.

Peanut Butter Jelly stood up on his hind legs and looked back at us with bright blue and green eyes he didn't have before. "This whole night was weird," he said. "Foxes can't talk."

THE END

Did you miss how I first met Fox? It all started when **My Fox Ate My Homework**. Read it now and then see what happened when **My Fox Ate My Cake**.

You can keep up with everything I'm doing and get more information about my stories at **www.davidblazebooks.com**

And you can follow me on Facebook at **https://www.facebook.com/davidblazeauthor** . Be sure to like the page so you know what me and Fox are up to.

The name David Blaze was envisioned by Timothy David for his son, Zander Blaze, to create a world for him and all children that is fun, safe, enlightening, hilarious, and honest. Wow! That's awesome!

If you enjoyed my story, please tell your friends and family. I'd also appreciate it if you'd leave a review on Amazon.com and tell me what you think about my best friend, Fox.

DAVID BLAZE

Made in the USA
Middletown, DE
02 January 2018